STORYBOTS

T0353956

WHY ARE BIRTHDAYS SPECIAL?

By Scott Emmons
Illustrated by Taylor Price

 A GOLDEN BOOK • NEW YORK

rhcbooks.com
ISBN 978-0-593-48331-2 (trade) — ISBN 978-0-593-48332-9 (ebook)
Printed in the United States of America
10 9 8 7 6 5 4 3 2 1

"That's true," the sun answered. "A year is the time it takes for the Earth to go all the way around me, or *orbit* me. Let's say you were born on March 1. When the Earth completes one orbit, it's March 1 again, but a year later. And that's your birthday!"

"That's right!" said Earth as she came spinning by. "For me, a year is 365 days. So when someone has a birthday, it's been 365 days since the last one!"

"Cool!" said Bang. "But is that all there is to it? Does a birthday just mean you've gone around again?"

"Well," said Earth, "365 days is a long time, and a lot happens in one trip around the sun. Here, I'll show you!"

Earth showed them a picture of children on a playground. "Here are some of the kids who live on me," she said. "Will they look the same a year from now?"

"No!" said Bing. "They'll be bigger!"

"That's right!" said Earth. "Here are the same kids a year later. They're bigger, yes, but they can also do things they couldn't do before. People keep growing and learning every year, so birthdays are a way to celebrate how far they've come."

"What about grown-ups?" asked Bo. "They stop growing, don't they?"

"True," said Earth. "But even though they don't get bigger every year, their minds keep growing because they learn new things. And that's something to celebrate!"

"I think we have our answer, guys,"
said Beep. "We know why birthdays are
special. Let's go back and tell Hap what
we've learned!"

When the StoryBots returned to Hap's office, he was working as hard as ever. "You again?" he snapped. "I told you, I don't have time for that birthday nonsense!"

"But it's not nonsense, Boss," said Beep. "We've learned why birthdays are special and why they're important to celebrate!"

"Yeah!" said Bing. "A birthday means the Earth has gone all the way around the sun, so you're one year older!"

"It takes 365 whole days!" said Bo.

"Totally!" Bang added. "That's 365 days of growing, learning, and, like, life experience, man."

"And that's why birthdays are special!" they all said.

"Boop!" agreed Boop.

Hap put down the phone. "You know what?" he said. "I've answered 365,000 questions in the last year. And I've learned a ton. That really *is* something to celebrate! Well, don't just stand there dillydallying. Let's have a party! Move! Move!"

For once, Hap took a break. He put on a party hat,
enjoyed his cake and ice cream, and opened lots of
presents. "Thank you, StoryBots!" he said.

"Our pleasure," they answered.